Abigail
the Breeze
Fairy

Dedicated to the real fairies who
make my garden grow.

Special thanks to
Sue Bentley

ISBN-13: 978-0-439-81386-0
ISBN-10: 0-439-81386-7

15   13 14 15 16/0
Printed in the U.S.A.

Abigail
the Breeze
Fairy

by Daisy Meadows

SCHOLASTIC INC.

New York   Toronto   London   Auckland   Sydney
Mexico City   New Delhi   Hong Kong   Buenos Aires

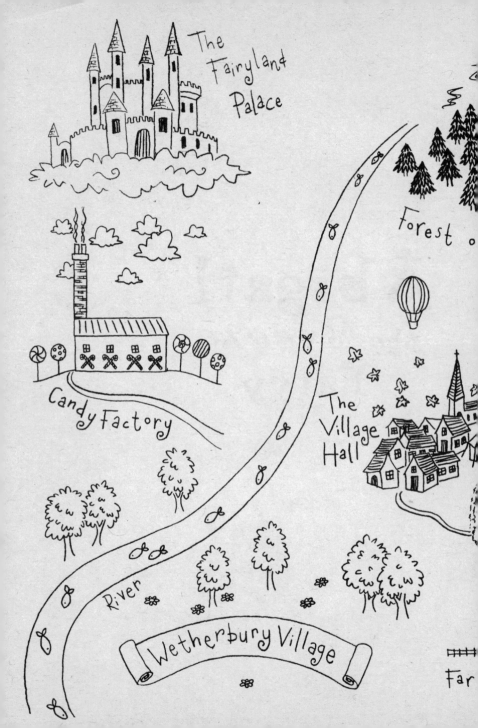

The Fairyland Palace

Candy Factory

Forest o

The Village Hall

River

Wetherbury Village

Far

Jack Frost's
Ice Castle

reen Wood

Mrs. Fordham's House

The Park

Willow Hill

High St.

The
Museum

irsty's
House

Fields

Mudhole

N
W E
S

Goblins green and goblins small,
I cast this spell to make you tall.
As high as the palace you shall grow.
My icy magic makes it so.

Then steal the rooster's magic feathers,
used by the fairies to make all weathers.
Climate chaos I have planned
on Earth, and here, in Fairyland!

Contents

The Adventure Begins

"I'm so glad I could come and stay with you!" Rachel Walker said happily. She sat with her friend, Kirsty Tate, in the garden outside Kirsty's house. The sun shone brightly on the green lawn and pretty flowering bushes.

"Me too," agreed Kirsty, smiling. "And it's very exciting to help the fairies again!"

1

Kirsty and Rachel had met while on vacation with their parents a few months earlier, and they'd had a wonderful fairy adventure. Jack Frost had cast a nasty spell to banish the seven Rainbow Fairies from Fairyland, and the girls had helped rescue them. With Rachel and Kirsty's help, the fairies were able to bring color back to Fairyland!

Now Jack Frost was causing even more trouble in Fairyland. He had ordered his goblin servants to steal the seven magic feathers from Doodle, the weather vane rooster. Doodle and the seven Weather Fairies were in charge of the weather in Fairyland. But without his magic tail feathers the rooster was powerless! Fairyland's weather would be all mixed up until Rachel and Kirsty could help the

Weather Fairies find all seven of Doodle's stolen feathers.

"I hope we find another magic feather today," said Rachel. She and Kirsty had already helped Crystal the Snow Fairy return the Snow Feather to Doodle.

The goblins were hiding all around Wetherbury, where Kirsty lived. And they had been up to lots of mischief, using the magic feathers to create some very unusual weather in the country village.

Kirsty looked anxious. "We still need to find six more feathers," she said. "Or poor Doodle will be stuck on top of our barn forever!" She glanced up at the roof of the old wooden barn. Here in the human world, the magical rooster was just a rusty metal weather vane.

Just then, a bush near the garden gate began to rustle. Kirsty and Rachel could see its pink flowers jiggling. "Do you think there's a goblin in that bush?" Kirsty whispered.

"Yes! I can see it moving." Rachel gasped. She was worried about facing another goblin. They were much scarier now that Jack Frost had cast a spell to make them bigger.

"Come on!" Kirsty said, running across the lawn. "He might have one of Doodle's feathers."

Rachel followed her, watching the bush nervously.

An angry screech came from the middle of the bush. Rachel and Kirsty looked at each other in surprise. Suddenly, two cats shot out and chased each other into the barn.

"Oh!" Kirsty exclaimed, and she and Rachel laughed with relief.

Just then, Kirsty's mom appeared at the front door. "There you are, Kirsty," she said. "Would you and Rachel like to go to the Summer Festival in the village? You can cheer your grandma on in the Cake Competition. She's hoping to win this year."

Kirsty and Rachel looked at each other and smiled. "We'd love to," Kirsty replied. "Gran makes the best cakes!"

Mrs. Tate laughed. "Yes, she does. But you'd better hurry if you want to get there before the judging starts."

A few minutes later, the girls were hurrying down Twisty Lane toward High Street. It was a beautiful day. Birds soared in the blue sky and wildflowers dotted the bushes like tiny jewels. As they walked by a thatched cottage with a pretty garden full of roses, a sharp gust of wind blew a shower of flower petals onto the sidewalk.

Just then, a large white envelope landed at Kirsty's feet. "Where did that

come from?" she murmured, and then
she gasped as more letters came spinning
and whirling toward her.

"The wind's really blowing hard now,"
Rachel said, stooping to pick up some of
the letters.

"Hey! Come back!" called a voice. A
mailman was running toward them,
chasing the envelopes that had been
carried away by the breeze.

The girls picked up the letters from the ground and handed them to the mailman. He grinned and stuffed them back into his bag.

"Thanks," he said. "This wind's really strong. Listen, it's even blowing the church bell now!"

He walked on to deliver his letters as Kirsty and Rachel hurried toward the festival. As they walked, they could hear the church bell clanging in the breeze.

The wind seemed to be getting stronger
and stronger. When the girls arrived at
the festival, they saw that the wind
was causing chaos there. Strings of flags
had come loose and were blowing in the
wind like kite tails. Three tents strained
against their ropes as they billowed and
swayed. Many of the stallholders had to

fight to stop their goods from blowing
away.

 With a loud snap, the side of a tent tore
free from its ropes and began flapping in
the wind. Some men ran over to tie it
back down. "I've never seen wind like
this in the middle of summer," one of
them complained.

As the girls headed off to look for the
Cake Competition, Kirsty noticed a small
boy struggling to hold on to a yellow
balloon. Suddenly, the wind whipped it
out of his hand.

"My balloon!" cried the boy.

"We'll catch it!" called Kirsty, already
running after the balloon.

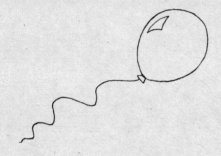

Rachel followed her friend. "There's something very strange about this wind!" she shouted.

"I know," puffed Kirsty, jumping up to catch the balloon's string. "Do you think it could be magic?"

The girls looked at each other, their eyes shining with excitement.

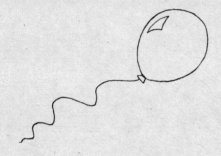

Cake Chaos!

Kirsty and Rachel caught the balloon
and took it back to the little boy, who
was standing outside one of the tents.
When he saw it, the boy's face lit up.
"My balloon!" He beamed. "Thank you."

"You're welcome," Kirsty replied.

Just then, she heard a familiar voice.

"Hello, Kirsty," called a plump, jolly-looking lady, as she hurried over to join the girls.

"Hi, Gran," Kirsty said. She turned to Rachel. "This is my dad's mom, Grandma Tate," she explained.

"Hello, Mrs. Tate," said Rachel. She glanced at the huge cake tin that Kirsty's gran held in her hands. "Is that the cake you're entering in the competition?"

Kirsty's gran nodded. "It's a chocolate fudge cake," she said. "That grumpy Mrs. Adelstrop always wins the competition. But I think I have a chance this year."

"Who's Mrs. Adelstrop?" Rachel asked.

Just then, another woman with a cake tin pushed by. "Out of my way!" she demanded. "This wind is terrible!" With that, she disappeared inside a nearby tent.

"I'll bet you've guessed who that was," whispered Kirsty's gran.

"Mrs. Adelstrop!" the girls replied.

"You got it right on the first try," said Gran with a laugh. "Well, I have to go get ready now. See you girls soon!" And she followed Mrs. Adelstrop into the tent.

"Good luck," called Rachel.

"Should we go inside, too?" Kirsty asked. "The goblin with the Breeze Feather must be close by. He might even be hiding inside the tent."

Rachel nodded and the girls wandered into the tent. A tall, thin man with a notepad stood behind a table full of delicious-looking cakes.

Mrs. Adelstrop smiled confidently and placed an enormous lemon cake on the table.

"That looks pretty good," Kirsty whispered, noticing the sugared lemon slices on top.

But then Kirsty's gran took out her chocolate fudge cake. Layers of chocolate sponge and buttercream filling were topped with icing and chocolate leaves. Mrs. Adelstrop's smile faded when she saw it.

"Wow! That's Gran's best cake ever!" Kirsty exclaimed happily.

"It looks delicious," Rachel agreed.

But as Mrs. Tate stepped forward to place her cake on the table, a huge gust of wind blew in through the entrance of the tent. A colored rope covered with flags snaked into the tent and wrapped itself around her legs.

Mrs. Tate stumbled, and the cake flew out of her hands. It sailed through the air and landed — *splat* — right in the judge's face!

Kirsty's gran looked horrified.
"Oh, how awful! Look at that poor
judge," she whispered to the girls.
"And there go my chances of winning
the Cake Competition this year!" she
added sadly.

"What an awful accident," said Mrs.
Adelstrop loudly. Kirsty could tell she was
trying not to look happy.

The judge stood there, covered in chocolate icing, as everyone rushed to help him clean up. The sound of the howling wind surrounded the tent, and the canvas flapped loudly.

"The wind's getting worse," whispered Rachel. "Let's see if the goblin is hiding under the table."

Kirsty lifted a corner of the tablecloth and peeked underneath, but there was no sign of a goblin.

Rachel glanced around the tent, looking for other possible goblin hiding places. Her eyes fell on a pretty fairy decoration, perched on top of a cake. Suddenly, she gasped. The tiny fairy was waving at her!

Goblin Discovered

The fairy's bright green eyes sparkled
with laughter. She wore a pretty yellow
top and a matching skirt with a little
green leaf on it. Her long brown hair
was tangled and windswept, and she held
an emerald-green wand with a shining

golden tip. Little bursts of golden leaves swirled from the tip of her wand.

Rachel's eyes widened. "Kirsty! Over here!" she whispered.

Kirsty hurried over. "It's Abigail the Breeze Fairy," she said happily. She and Rachel had met Abigail and all the other Weather Fairies in Fairyland.

"Hello, Rachel and Kirsty!" Abigail said, smiling. She twirled in the air in a cloud of gold-green dust and tiny bronze leaves.

"Thank goodness we've found you," said Rachel. "We think there's a goblin nearby."

Abigail's tiny face paled. "Goblins are nasty things — so big and scary! But we have to find this one," she said bravely, "before he causes any more trouble with the Breeze Feather." She fluttered her glittering wings and swooped onto Rachel's shoulder to hide underneath her hair.

"Well, the goblin isn't in this tent," said Kirsty. "Let's go outside and check the booths."

"Good idea," Rachel agreed, and the two friends left the tent, struggling against the blustery wind. They hadn't gotten far when they heard a loud creaking noise. Suddenly, the tent behind them collapsed! The girls saw Kirsty's gran rushing to help others, who were crawling out from beneath the canvas.

"Oh, what a mess!" said Rachel.

"At least it doesn't look like anyone's hurt," Kirsty pointed out.

The wind moaned loudly through a group of oak trees nearby. The branches thrashed back and forth, and green leaves rained down.

Abigail's tiny mouth drooped. "Poor trees. It's too soon for them to lose their leaves," she said sadly.

"This is more goblin mischief!" fumed Kirsty. "If that goblin keeps using the Breeze Feather, he'll tear the leaves off all the trees."

Quickly, the girls searched the tents and some of the stalls, but they didn't have any luck at all finding the goblin — or the Breeze Feather.

Then, Kirsty heard a dog barking. "It's Twiglet," she said, pointing at a cute Jack Russell puppy next to the raffle booth. "His owner is one of our neighbors, Mr. McDougall."

"We haven't searched the raffle booth yet," Rachel said. "Let's go and check there for goblins."

The girls hurried over. "Hello," Kirsty greeted her neighbor.

"Hello, my dear," said Mr. McDougall. "I don't think Twiglet likes this windstorm."

Kirsty nodded. She bent down to pet Twiglet, and the puppy jumped up from beside his empty food bowl. He wagged his tail and wiggled his little nose. Kirsty stroked his soft, floppy ears. "You're gorgeous," she said, smiling.

"What's that?" Rachel asked, pointing to a torn piece of material in Twiglet's mouth.

Kirsty pulled the material away from Twiglet. It was brown leather and it smelled moldy.

Rachel and Kirsty looked at it closely.

"I'm sure I've seen something like this before," Rachel said thoughtfully. "I wonder where Twiglet got it."

Suddenly, Twiglet began barking again. He was staring up at the sky, and jumping up and down.

"That's odd," said Mr. McDougall. "He keeps doing that. I wonder why."

"Maybe he's hungry?" suggested Rachel.

Mr. McDougall shook his head. "Can't be. His dish is empty. He must have eaten all of his food when I wasn't looking."

Twiglet snapped and growled, still looking upward. The girls and Abigail followed the puppy's gaze toward the sky.

"Look at that!" Rachel pointed to a hot-air balloon floating in the sky above the festival. The balloon was covered with red and orange stripes, and a large basket hung down from it. The fierce wind sent leaves and bits of paper whirling around it, but the balloon itself seemed to hang in midair without moving. A bright spurt of flame shot from the burner to heat the air in the balloon and keep it floating.

"That's strange," said Kirsty. "It doesn't seem to be affected by the wind at all!"

"Yes," Rachel agreed. "How can it stay so still with the wind blowing all around it?"

"The goblin must be hiding in it!"

Abigail exclaimed. "Only the magic Breeze Feather could protect the balloon from the wind like that."

Kirsty's eyes widened. "So we've finally found the goblin," she said. "But he's way up in the sky!"

Up, Up, and Away!

"How are we going to get up there?" Rachel asked.

"Easy!" Abigail told her. "We use fairy magic!"

The girls immediately reached for their shining golden lockets. The lockets were full of magic fairy dust. They had been special gifts from Titania, the Fairy Queen. A pinch of the dust would turn the girls into fairies, and another pinch would turn them back into humans again.

Rachel sprinkled herself with sparkling fairy dust, then laughed with delight as she shrank to fairy size. The grass was as tall as she was, and the buttercups now seemed as big as trees!

Kirsty did the same, and turned around to look at her silvery wings. "Wow! I'm a fairy again!"

"We have to hurry!" Abigail said, zooming up into the air.

She was quickly followed by Kirsty and
Rachel.

The higher Abigail and the girls
flew, the more the
wind tried to blow
them off course.
Kirsty and Rachel's
wings soon felt
really tired.

"Fly right
behind me,"
Abigail urged the
girls. "It might be
easier for you."

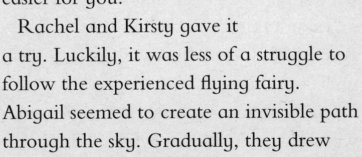

Rachel and Kirsty gave it
a try. Luckily, it was less of a struggle to
follow the experienced flying fairy.
Abigail seemed to create an invisible path
through the sky. Gradually, they drew

closer and closer to the balloon's basket.

"We were right. Look!" cried Kirsty.

An ugly face peered over the edge of the balloon's basket. It was a goblin with pointed ears and a big, lumpy nose.

"He's a very big goblin," said Abigail nervously.

"I don't think he's seen us yet," Rachel whispered. "Let's creep up behind him."

The goblin was staring at Twiglet, who was still barking down below. "Ha, ha!

Silly little doggy. You can't catch me!" he sneered.

Kirsty and Rachel heard the goblin's tummy rumble. It sounded like mud being stirred in a bucket. The goblin gave a huge burp, and a blast of stinky breath blew over Rachel, Kirsty, and Abigail.

"Ugh!" Abigail held her nose.

"What a terrible smell!" complained Rachel. "What has that goblin been eating?"

"Can't catch me, doggy!" The goblin
continued to taunt Twiglet, jumping up
and down and waving a shining bronze
feather.

Down on the ground, a strong gust of
wind swept Twiglet off his feet. The
puppy tumbled over, got up again, and
shook his head angrily. Then he looked
up and began barking even more loudly.

The goblin jumped back, surprised. Then he recovered. "I'm safe up here!" he said to himself, and laughed.

Rachel was confused. *The goblin's afraid of Twiglet,* she thought. *I wonder why.*

"He's holding the Breeze Feather!" whispered Abigail. Her leaf-green eyes flashed with anger.

"Yes. And he's using it to tease poor Twiglet!" said Kirsty. "What a mean goblin! We have to get that feather back."

Rachel was thinking hard. "I've got a plan," she told her friends. "Kirsty, you land in the basket. Then Abigail can make you human-size, and the two of you can distract the goblin while I fly up and turn off the balloon's burner. The balloon will sink, and we'll have a better chance of getting the feather back once that goblin's back on the ground."

"That's a good idea," said Abigail. "But Kirsty and I will be very close to the goblin. Can you be quick, Rachel?"

"I will," Rachel promised.

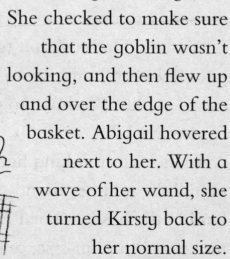

"Okay, then here I go," Kirsty said. She checked to make sure that the goblin wasn't looking, and then flew up and over the edge of the basket. Abigail hovered next to her. With a wave of her wand, she turned Kirsty back to her normal size.

When he saw Kirsty, the goblin's eyes grew as big as golf balls. "Who are you?" he demanded.

"I'm Kirsty, a friend of the Weather Fairies," Kirsty declared firmly.

"And I'm Abigail the Breeze Fairy," Abigail added in her soft, musical voice.

The goblin glared at Abigail. "Boo!" he shouted, and lunged at her.

Abigail fluttered out of his reach, and the goblin snorted with laughter.

Just then, Kirsty saw Rachel overhead, turning off the burner. *So far so good*, she thought. *The goblin hasn't noticed Rachel.*

The goblin scowled at Kirsty. "Get off my balloon!" he roared.

"That's not very nice," Kirsty said calmly.

"I don't care!" snapped the goblin. He looked at Abigail slyly. "I know what you want and you're not going to get it!" he said, waving the Breeze Feather.

A huge gust of wind rocked the basket. Kirsty clung to the side as it tilted and wobbled.

The goblin snickered. "Too windy for you?"

"Your balloon's sinking," Kirsty answered.

"Don't be ridiculous!" sneered the goblin. Then he looked over the edge of the basket. "What?"

47

Down below, but getting closer all the time, Twiglet barked and growled.

The goblin's big nose twitched nervously.

Kirsty noticed a rip in the goblin's ragged clothing and remembered the piece of material in Twiglet's mouth. "Why are you afraid of the puppy?" she asked.

The goblin looked shifty. "I might have eaten his dinner," he replied sulkily.

No wonder his breath is so stinky! thought Kirsty.

"Now, tell me why this balloon's sinking!" demanded the goblin fiercely. "Or I'll wave the Breeze Feather and tip you out of the basket — like this!"

The basket rocked back and forth. Kirsty's heart pounded, but she hung on to the side. The goblin hardly moved, even though the basket shook and wobbled. He was perfectly balanced on his big, broad feet. He waved the Breeze Feather again, making the basket rock more than ever.

Kirsty reached nervously for her fairy locket. She would need her fairy wings if she was tipped out of the basket. But would she have time to use the fairy dust if she fell?

Flying High

"There's too much weight in this
basket! That's why we're sinking," said
Abigail.

The goblin glared at Kirsty. "You're
too heavy. Get out!" he ordered.

Quick as a flash, Kirsty sprinkled
herself with fairy dust from her locket
and fluttered out of the goblin's way.

"We're still sinking!" the goblin cried.

Suddenly, his ugly face brightened. "But I don't need these heavy sandbags. They just help the balloon to land," he said. He grabbed the sandbags that hung around the edge of the basket and heaved them over the side. To his dismay, the balloon continued to sink lower and lower. "What will I do?" he wailed.

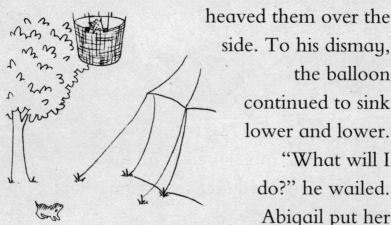

Abigail put her hands on her hips. "You'll have to throw out that feather!" she told the goblin firmly.

"No!" snapped the goblin. "It's mine, and I'm keeping it! Besides, it's too light to make any difference."

Kirsty and Rachel hovered in the air
behind Abigail. Would she be able to
convince the goblin to get rid of the
feather?

"It's a lot heavier
than you think,"
Abigail said.

The goblin
scowled. "What do
you mean?"

"A pound of feathers weighs
just the same as a pound of
rocks, you know," Abigail replied.

Kirsty and Rachel laughed softly. *They*
knew that a pound of anything weighs
just the same as a pound of anything else!
But goblins are foolish, and the girls
guessed that Abigail was hoping to
confuse this one.

The goblin blinked and scratched his head. Abigail's plan was working!

On the ground below, Twiglet barked and jumped up at the balloon. He seemed a lot closer now.

"Argh! Don't let it get me!" screamed the goblin. And in desperation, he flung the feather out of the basket. Abigail flew after it in a blur of golden wings, but the feather was caught by the wind and swept away.

"Come on!" shouted Rachel, flying after Abigail. Kirsty followed.

"The wind's too strong. I can't fly!" cried Rachel in panic.

The girls were tossed around by the wind. They flapped their wings and tried to regain control, but it was no use. They were drifting farther and farther from the Breeze Feather, and they couldn't even see Abigail through all the leaves and garbage swirling around them.

"We have to catch the Breeze Feather," shouted Kirsty. "Otherwise it could be lost forever!"

Bright and Breezy

Suddenly, Kirsty and Rachel caught a glimpse of Abigail flying to their rescue.

"Don't worry about us," Kirsty shouted above the wind.

"Just catch the Breeze Feather!" Rachel yelled.

Abigail must have heard them, because she nodded firmly and sped off after the feather again. She seemed about to grab it, when the wind snatched it away from her. Rachel let out a cry, but then she saw a rope of tiny golden leaves snake out from Abigail's wand and wrap around the Breeze Feather.

The tiny fairy pulled the feather toward her and finally managed to grab hold of it. She immediately waved it in a complicated pattern. "Wind, stop!" she ordered.

With a soft sigh, the roaring wind died.
Kirsty and Rachel could immediately fly
properly again.

Abigail flew over to join them. "It's
wonderful to have the Breeze Feather
back safe and sound!" she said happily.

"What about the goblin?"
asked Kirsty.

Abigail frowned.
"Leave him to
me!" She
pointed the
feather at
the hot-air
balloon. "Wind,
blow!" she
commanded. An
enormous puff of
wind rocked the balloon.

The goblin hung over the basket. His face looked green. "I feel sick," he moaned.

"You shouldn't have eaten Twiglet's dinner, then!" Rachel told him.

"I wish I hadn't," replied the goblin gloomily. "It wasn't very good, anyway!"

Abigail waved the Breeze Feather a second time and the big red-and-orange balloon blew high into the sky. The goblin's cries faded as the balloon flew out of sight.

Kirsty, Rachel, and
Abigail flew to the
festival and slid
down one of the
tents to the ground.
Abigail waved her
wand, and Kirsty and
Rachel grew back to their
normal size. They peeked out

from behind the tent.
Now that the wind
had stopped,
people were
running around
organizing their
stalls. Over on
the lawn, Twiglet
was chewing
contentedly.

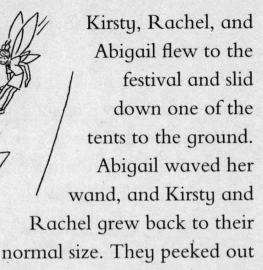

"Mr. McDougall gave Twiglet a dog biscuit to chew on," said Kirsty.

"I bet it tastes better than that goblin's clothes!" laughed Rachel.

"Kirsty!" called Kirsty's gran.

Abigail quickly zoomed onto Kirsty's shoulder and hid beneath her hair.

"Gran!" Suddenly, Kirsty remembered what had happened to her gran's cake. So why was her gran wearing such a big smile?

"I won first prize!" said Mrs. Tate, her eyes shining. "The judge said my cake was delicious. He couldn't help tasting it when it was all over his face!"

The girls were just congratulating Mrs. Tate when Mrs. Adelstrop stomped past, scowling.

Kirsty's gran chuckled. "She's won first prize for the last three years. It's time someone else had a chance!"

Rachel and Kirsty laughed. And only they heard the silvery giggling that came from under Kirsty's hair.

"Now I have to go," said Gran. "My best friend, Mable, is hoping to win a prize in one of the vegetable competitions!"

Kirsty and Rachel waved good-bye.

"We should go and give Doodle his magic feather back," said Kirsty.

The girls and Abigail headed home.

It was quiet and sunny now, and a warm summer breeze gently rustled through the leaves on Twisty Lane. "Everything's back to normal," said Rachel happily.

"For now," Kirsty added.

Back at Kirsty's house, Abigail flew straight up to the barn roof and carefully put the Breeze Feather into Doodle's tail.

The weather vane rooster shimmered in a magic haze of gold. And then he fizzed into life and shook himself. Fabulous copper sparkles flew into the air, making Rachel and Kirsty gasp. Doodle's fiery feathers were magnificent.

Doodle shifted to settle the Breeze Feather properly into place, where it glimmered and glowed. Then he looked straight at Rachel and Kirsty. "Jack —" he squawked, and opened his beak as if to speak again, but the color of his feathers faded. Doodle became a rusty old weather vane once more.

"He's trying to tell us something," said Kirsty.

"Last time, he said 'Beware,'" Rachel reminded Kirsty. "So now we have 'Beware Jack. . . .' I wonder what he wanted to say next?"

Abigail floated down from the roof. "I don't know," she said. "But keep your eyes open. Jack Frost is always up to no good."

"We will," Kirsty promised.

"Now I must fly back to Fairyland," Abigail said. "Thank you again, Rachel and Kirsty."

"Good-bye, Abigail!" Kirsty said, and Rachel waved.

Abigail's wings flashed, and with a swirl of tiny golden leaves, she was gone.

Rachel and Kirsty smiled at each other, enjoying their fairy secret.

"Five more magic feathers to find!" whispered Kirsty.

"I wonder which one we'll find next," Rachel said.

THE WEATHER FAIRIES

Now that Abigail has her weather
feather back, Rachel and Kirsty
must help

Pearl

the Cloud Fairy!

Join their next adventure
in this special sneak peek!

Missing Fidget

"What's the weather like today, Kirsty?" asked Rachel Walker eagerly. She pushed back her bedspread. "Do you think there's magic in the air?"

Kirsty Tate was standing at the bedroom window, staring out over the garden. "It seems like a normal day."

She sighed, with a disappointed look on her face. "The sky's gray and cloudy."

"Never mind." Rachel jumped out of bed and went to join her friend. "Remember what Titania, the Fairy Queen, told us. Don't look too hard for magic —"

"Because the magic will find you!" Kirsty finished with a smile.

"Morning, you two," said Mr. Tate with a smile, as the girls sat down to breakfast. "What are you planning to do today?"

Before Kirsty or Rachel could answer him, there was a knock at the back door.

"I'll get it," said Kirsty.

She opened the door. There were Mr. and Mrs. Twitching, the Tates' neighbors.

"Oh, Kirsty, good morning," said Mr. Twitching. "We're sorry to bother you, but we were hoping you might have seen Fidget?"

Kirsty frowned, trying to remember. She knew Fidget, the Twitchings' fluffy tabby cat, very well, but she hadn't seen her for the last day or two. "I haven't seen her lately," she replied.

"Oh, dear," Mrs. Twitching said, looking upset. "She didn't come home for her dinner last night."

As Mr. and Mrs. Twitching walked into the kitchen, Kirsty blinked. For a minute, she thought she'd seen strange wisps of pale smoke curling and drifting over the neighbors' heads.

She glanced at Rachel and her parents, but they didn't seem to have noticed anything unusual. Kirsty shook her head. Maybe she was just imagining it. . . .

RAINBOW magic™

There's Magic in Every Series!

The Rainbow Fairies
The Weather Fairies
The Jewel Fairies
The Pet Fairies
The Fun Day Fairies
The Petal Fairies
The Dance Fairies
The Music Fairies
The Sports Fairies
The Party Fairies
The Ocean Fairies
The Night Fairies
The Magical Animal Fairies
The Princess Fairies
The Superstar Fairies

Read them all!